GINGER GREEN
on the
(UN)LUCKIEST Camp EVER!

Ginger Green on the (Un)luckiest Camp Ever!
published in 2018 by
Hardie Grant Egmont
Ground Floor, Building 1, 658 Church Street
Richmond, Victoria 3121, Australia
www.hardiegrantegmont.com

 A catalogue record for this
book is available from the
National Library of Australia

Text copyright © 2018 Kim Kane
Illustrations copyright © 2018 Jon Davis
Series design copyright © 2018 Hardie Grant Egmont

Design by Stephanie Spartels
Typesetting by Kristy Lund-White

Printed in Australia by McPherson's Printing Group,
Maryborough, Victoria.

1 3 5 7 9 10 8 6 4 2

 The paper in this book is FSC® certified.
FSC® promotes environmentally responsible,
socially beneficial and economically viable
management of the world's forests.

GINGER GREEN
on the (UN)LUCKIEST Camp EVER!

BY KIM KANE
& JON DAVIS

Hardie Grant
EGMONT

For my friend Kristen, with whom
I first learnt to write, and for Astrid,
a first contributor and first fan.

– Kim

For Laura and Greta.

– Jon

CHAPTER 1

'My name is **GINGER!** Ginger Green.'

I am eight years old.

When I was in grade two,
I was **really** into play dates.
Now that I am in grade three,
I am still into play dates
but I am also into **bigger**
kid things.

I can drink a **hot** hot chocolate.

I am old enough to stay up and watch **both** halves of the footy.

I can see over the counter at Kotch Lane Cafe ...

that one!

$2 EACH

2 FOR 1

2

and I am **finally** big enough to go on

SCHOOL CAMP.

→

I have been counting down the days since term one!

3

Today, grade three is going to
STAR GLEN RANCH.

Star Glen Ranch is two hours away by bus.

Star Glen Ranch sounds like it might have

cowboys. It sounds like it might

even have **horse-riding**.

I am hoping it at least
has **WILD BUFFALO**
and **LASSOS.**   yee haw!

4

Mum bought me a new **BIG BAG** for camp.

It is **bright green** with wheels and a handle. It has two pouches. The top part fits my sleeping bag, a sheet and my pillow and the bottom part fits my clothes.

It even has a side zip for a torch.

Everything I'm taking to camp,
including my bag, is **LABELLED**.

Everything is labelled

GINGER GREEN

or even

VIOLET GREEN

because Violet is my big sister
and I always get her

hand-me-downs.

NOTHING is labelled

PENNY GREEN.

Penny is my younger sister and she hasn't been on camp yet. I hope that when Penny does go on camp at least **something** is labelled PENNY GREEN. It probably won't be clothes because Mum and Dad might have got **fed up** and just stopped buying them for her by then.

But we could always label something like the PILLOW or her UNDIES.

Mum, Dad and I have been sewing on nametags **EVERY NIGHT THIS WEEK**. Mum says she hopes she **NEVER** sees another nametag again.

Dad is excellent at sewing.

Dad is a doctor like Mum, only he sews up people. Mum checks freckles and moles instead.

Because he has had so much practice at sewing up people, Dad also sews on labels **better than anyone**.

That is a thing most people don't know about doctors. So if you ever get your tonsils out at the hospital, take along your latest craft project **and just see what happens.**

I know all about tonsils because when my best friend, Lottie, was sick for my birthday party, she had tonsillitis. And now Lottie is sick for school camp because she is having her tonsils out.

Yep. My **best friend** has already been away from school for one whole week and there is **NO WAY** she is allowed to go on camp.

'It is a TRAGEDY,'

I say to Mum.

'Poor Lottie,' says Mum. 'At least this way, those tonsils won't get in her way again.'

When we get to school, the buses are waiting.

They are lined up along the street.

I did not think I would feel nervous,
but I **DO** feel **VERY** nervous.

That surprises me.

On school camp you spend lots
of time with your friends.
I love my friends.
But now that Lottie is sick, I am worried that
I won't be in a cabin with my friends and I will
have to sleep with kids I don't really know.

And I am worried that the broccoli will be cooked so it is **GREY AND MUSHY**  and I won't be able to leave the table until I eat it.

yuck!

And I am worried that the rooms will have SPIDERS because when Violet went on camp she found a

MASSIVE SPIDER

under her bed and also a

DIRTY OLD SOCK,

which was not as bad as the spider but still not great.

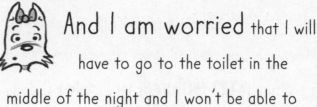 And I am worried that I will have to go to the toilet in the middle of the night and I won't be able to remember where the toilet is. And I am VERY worried I will end up **WEEING IN THE SHOWER OR JUST PLAIN WETTING THE BED**. And I am worried that even though my family usually drives me nuts, especially my sisters, I will miss them. A lot.

I know that camp only goes for one night and I know that I should not be nervous. But I am. I have a bag of worries as big as my camp bag.

Mum helps me line up my camp bag to put it in the boot under the bus. We line it up next to Daya's bag. Daya is my tiny **(but definitely not cute)** friend. Daya is small but **VERY VERY LOUD.**

I check the zip on my bag to make sure it is closed properly. Daya does the same. Daya's bag is bigger than she is.

'Big bag,' I say.

'I can actually fit in it,' says Daya.

She is lying down on top of the bag.

'If the beds are uncomfy, I'll just sleep in my bag.

Or on it!' Daya is little but she is practical like that.

very!

I laugh as the bus doors open.

Daya makes me laugh.

As I laugh, my bag of worries shrinks.

It doesn't disappear but I can suddenly

let myself be a bit excited again.

I kiss Mum and climb onto the bus. I stare down the aisle. **I am Ginger Green**, I think, and I have lots of friends. When it comes to the bus, though, I wish I had just one friend. One best friend. One bus friend. Like Lottie. Or Daya. As Lottie is not here, I want to sit with Daya.

I want to sit with Daya because she is chatty and that is just what I feel like when I am still a bit nervous. But Meagan has already bossed me into sitting with her. Meagan is clever so she already worked out last week that she would need a bus friend and that Lottie was sick and would not be going on camp. Meagan is organised like that.

Meagan is already on the bus.

'Ginger! Ginger! Here!'

Meagan is slapping the empty seat next to her. She has saved me a seat **right at the FRONT**.

'We're **VERY** close to the teachers,'

I say.

'We're very close to the movie,'

says Meagan, and points to a small TV screen.

I smile, mainly to be polite, and sit next to Meagan. I am feeling a bit annoyed, though. **A BIT BOSSED.** I really did feel like sitting next to Daya even if Daya is right down the back and won't see one single thing except the headrest in front of her.

After Ms Marinelli checks the roll and gives us all nametags, the bus starts moving and all the parents wave. We drive for two whole hours and the teachers don't even turn on the TV. Instead, we sing the entire the way to camp. I sing loudly.

I sing VERY loudly.

We sing

'NINETY-NINE BOTTLES OF JUICE ON THE WALL!'

We sing and we sing all the way down
to twenty-three bottles of juice.

'That's seventy-six bottles down,' says Meagan.

I LOOK PUZZLED.

'Ninety-nine minus twenty-three is seventy-six,
Ginger. I know you are good at times tables
but you **REALLY** do need to work
on your mental maths,'
she says.

I sing louder.

Meagan stops singing the tune and starts to sing lower. Meagan sings the line 'Twenty-three bottles of juice on the wall' in **perfect harmony**.

'How do you know the harmony?' I ask. 'Do you sing the harmony at home?'

'I have never heard this song,' says Meagan.
'We only listen to **classical radio** at my
house, but I do know all about harmony.'

Meagan explains why the harmony works.

Meagan knows all about music theory.

Meagan goes
ON AND ON.

Eyeroll!

'Why don't you sing it rather than talk about it?'
I whisper. I have to admit Meagan has a pretty
voice. I also have to admit I do not really want to
hear about music theory on the bus.
I just want to shout out the words.

Finally, after **TWO HOURS** and
NINETY-NINE BOTTLES OF JUICE,
including some in perfect harmony, we turn into
STAR GLEN RANCH.

Star Glen Ranch is quite dusty and the grass is very dry. There are some trees and picnic tables and a few long, low buildings. Cabins sit up on top of a big, tall hill, all in a row like birds on a telephone wire.

To the left of the hill, there is a lake and beyond that some bush with ropes and ladders.

STAR GLEN RANCH

Meagan leans over me and points.

'That's the obstacle course,' she says.

'Star Glen Ranch is famous for it.

It is very **HIGH** and very **CHALLENGING**.'

I have not heard of the obstacle course.

I do not know what an obstacle course is.

I just know that I do not see a single horse.

I do not see a single cowboy. yee haw?

I do not see a single buffalo.

'I thought a ranch was for **horse-riding**,' I say.

Meagan shakes her head. 'It is, but this ranch is just an obstacle course.'

'Oh,' I whisper.

Camp is **NOT** turning out how I thought it would **AT ALL.**

CHAPTER 2

I do not, however, have time to
think too much about how camp was
supposed to be. Ms Marinelli jumps
up from her seat with a clipboard.

It is funny seeing
teachers on camp.
**The teachers
are all in
tracksuits.**

I am not used to seeing my teachers
in tracksuits. I am used to seeing
them in smart pants or skirts.

A few of the other teachers have unloaded all the bags. They sit in a **BIG DUSTY PILE** in the car park. I find my bag, which is actually quite tricky even though I am the only kid whose bag is **bright green**.

We lug our stuff up the hill to the cabins.

The hill is high.

The hill is steep.

Much steeper than it looked.

I am glad my new bag is green and I am glad it has wheels. Some kids are trying to carry sports bags and plastic bags and pillows and soft toys.

Maisy has a **HOLE** in her bag and has dropped **SOCKS**, **UNDIES**, **T-SHIRTS** and her face washer on the grass.

I leave my bag near the cabins and run back down the hill to help Maisy pick everything up. Martha does front **WALKOVERS** beside me. She goes over and over like a windmill. 'I'll help too,' she says.

Martha is my BENDY FRIEND, my bendiest friend actually.

Once we had a play date in the supermarket and Martha pushed a shopping trolley **with her toes,** just before she broke her arm. Luckily her arm is all fixed now so she doesn't have to wear a cast.

Martha passes right by Maisy's gear and keeps doing **WALKOVERS,**

OVER AND OVER.

I guess it is hard to stop once you are in a loop.

I start to pick up Maisy's clothes and hand them to her.

'Better to see your undies on the grass than on the roof,' I say. When Maisy came over to my house for a play date, she ended up dancing in her **UNDIES** on our roof.

I would be **EMBARRASSED** if everybody saw my undies. Maisy does not care who sees her undies at all.

Maisy shrugs.

Maisy is staring at Martha. Martha is now lying on the grass and staring at the sky. 'Martha is **amazing** at gymnastics,' says Maisy.

I hand Maisy her plastic bag. 'She is,' I say. Then I say something else so Maisy can't get too distracted. When Maisy gets an idea in her head there is no telling where she could end up. 'Let's go to the top of the hill and see if you and Martha are in a cabin together.'

'Great idea,' says Maisy.

I smile. I smile because as IF a teacher would ever put Maisy and Martha in a cabin together.

as if!

I mean, they are both kind and fun, but they are both kind, fun and

WILD.

Much too wild to share a cabin.

At the top of the hill, there is a big list of all the cabins tacked to a wall.

'Am I with you, Ginger? Am I with you?' asks Meagan.

Meagan is a bit puffed from the steep uphill walk. I try to smile at Meagan. I do not want to be unkind to Meagan but I also do not really want to be in a cabin with her. I do not want to learn about music harmonies on camp. Although it has to be said that Meagan would be good for cabin points. The teachers are awarding points to each cabin for good behaviour. They are also taking them away when kids are badly behaved.

I look at the list. 'I am in CABIN FOUR.'

'Not so good for cabin points,' says Meagan.

I blink.
My mouth is tight.

I ended up with all my 'M' friends.

I ended up with **BOSSY BUT CLEVER** Meagan,

BENDY BUT BREAKABLE Martha,

and **MAD** Maisy with her undies on the grass.

Who on earth put **MAISY** and **MARTHA** in the **SAME CABIN?**

I think.

This is not an easy cabin.

This will not be good for cabin points.

In fact, this will be a **DISASTER**.

How can this go well?

Ellie walks up to check her cabin buddies, but she's really checking **MY** cabin buddies. Ellie is like that.

'Ooooh, you're in cabin **FOUR**.

Four is an **UNLUCKY** number in Chinese,' she says. 'The Chinese word for "four" sounds like the word for "**DEATH**". My grandmother won't let us buy a house with the number four in the address.'

'Thanks Ellie,'

I say.

'That is helpful. Lucky we're not on camp in China.'

'I'm in cabin eight. Eight is a lucky number,' says Ellie.

I pick up my bag and look at Ellie. Ellie is walking across to cabin eight with Maya and Yassmine and Daya. I want to murder Ellie.

I take a deep breath and walk along the path to cabin four. **THE CABIN OF BAD LUCK. THE CABIN OF DEATH.**

I walk with Martha. As usual, Martha is walking on her hands. Martha is pushing her bag with her toes.

Even if four is not an unlucky number, I think, **this is not going to end well.** There is no way this is going to end without a broken bone or lost glasses or a lost girl on the roof, possibly in her undies. **NO WAY AT ALL.**

'Martha Barber. Walking on your hands,'

says Ms Marinelli. Ms Marinelli does that.

She always says what you're doing wrong just before she launches into the punishment.

They must teach you that at teacher's school.

'Walking on your hands is forbidden. That's two cabin points off,' she says.

TWO CABIN POINTS OFF ALREADY?

We have lost cabin points and we haven't

even stepped foot in the cabin!

WE ARE ON MINUS TWO.

'We may not win the cabin points system,' warns Meagan in front of me.

'WIN?!' I say. 'I am just aiming to get back up to zero.'

Meagan doesn't say anything. I don't think Meagan likes to lose. I don't think Meagan has ever **NOT** won.

'Oh well. At least it won't be a BORE in cabin four,' I say.

It's not that I don't like the girls in my cabin. They are my friends. But I am a bit worried about them. I am worried about them because **I KNOW THEM**.

99 − 72 = 27

99
−33
66

I KNOW Meagan can be bossy even if she is kind. And I know *Meagan* knows that because Meagan knows *everything*.

I KNOW Martha spends most of her life upside down and has broken most of the bones you see on the skeleton in the museum.

I KNOW Maisy doesn't care who sees her undies and **I KNOW** she likes to climb. There are a lot of cabins and a lot of roofs at Star Glen Ranch.

There are a lot of roofs for Maisy to end up dancing on in her undies.

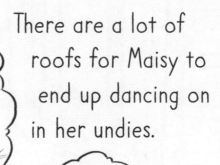

Our cabin is quite small but it has two sets of bunk beds. **Maisy will LOVE the bunk beds.** I can feel it in my bones.

There are four lockers in the room. I put my bag in the locker area. I throw my sheet onto the bottom bunk and pull out my sleeping bag. The mattresses are plastic and they are pretty squeaky.

Meagan's sheet and sleeping bag are already on her bed. Meagan's pillow and torch are too. I have to hand it to Meagan, she is fast and organised. No wonder her house was so neat before we ruined it when we had a play date.

Martha and Maisy have baggsed the top bunks.

I am not surprised.

They are both climbers after all.

Martha and Maisy have not unpacked their bags. They have not made their beds. They have not even started to make their beds. Their bags are right across the doorway.

Maisy and Martha are

BOUNCING

up and down on their bunk beds. They are not only bouncing up and down, they are jumping across the room and onto each other's bunk beds.

JUMP.

JUMP.

JUUUUUUUUUMP.

It actually looks pretty fun.

I forget all about cabin points.

I jump up onto Maisy's bunk too.

47

'We have a secret. We have a **SECRET**,' screams Maisy as she jumps.

I have **NO** idea what secret they're talking about.

'We have a secret. We have a **midnight** secret,' screams Martha as she jumps between the beds.

'Who cares about your secret?!' I shout. 'Let's pretend the rug is a river and the river is full of crocodiles. We are jumping from cliff to cliff. If we miss, we will tumble **DOWN DOWN DOWN** hundreds of metres ...'

'And die,' says Meagan.

'You will **break your necks** even if it is not a cliff and a river full of crocodiles but just a plain old bunk bed and a grotty rug.' Meagan has picked up her book. She is looking up at us through her glasses.

We ignore her.

Maisy leaps across the
river of death.
Martha

LEAPS

across the river and does a

SOMERSAULT

as she leaps.

Martha really is very
good at gymnastics.

I leap across the river.
I am **NOT** very good at gymnastics.

I leap my biggest leap
and land ...

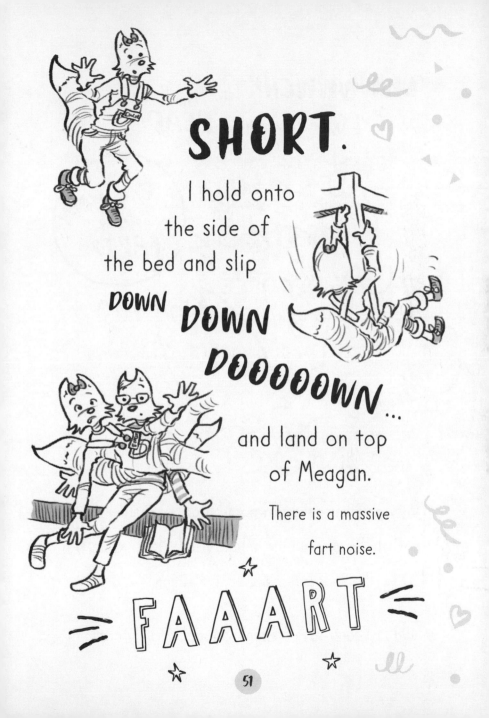

SHORT.

I hold onto the side of the bed and slip **DOWN** **DOWN** **DOOOOOWN**... and land on top of Meagan.

There is a massive fart noise.

FAAART

'OWWWWWCH!' screeches Meagan.
'I was trying to READ.'

'Did you do a **FART?'**

asks Maisy.

Maisy puts her head down and looks under the top bunk at Meagan and me. **Maisy loves a good fart.** 'That was a massive fart, Meagan.'

'I did not fart,' says Meagan. 'Most certainly not.'

Martha's head pops down next to Maisy's. 'I'm not sure you should say **FART**,' says Martha. 'It isn't very proper.'

'I can certainly *say* fart,' says Meagan. 'If it's good enough for Chaucer, it's good enough for me. Chaucer is the **FATHER** of English literature. But I did not *do* a fart. That was just the plastic mattress.'

'Oh,' says Maisy, and looks disappointed. Meagan does not seem like a big farter. I can see Maisy likes the thought that Meagan *could* be a big farter, though. It would make her more fun or something.

Ms Marinelli comes into the room.

As she walks in, she trips over Maisy and Martha's bags.

She falls flat on her bottom and
her scrunchy tracksuit pant legs go up in the air.
Just as Ms Marinelli falls, Meagan sits up and
her mattress makes another

MASSIVE FART.

Meagan laughs. Martha laughs.
Maisy laughs so hard
she falls down off
the top bunk ...
right next to
Ms Marinelli.

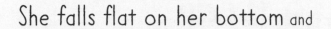

I rush to help Ms Marinelli.

Ms Marinelli ignores me. 'Monkeying around,' she says. She looks at Martha and me, and then across to Maisy. She looks at Martha and Maisy's unmade beds. She looks at my half-made bed. Now that Ms Marinelli has stated the **crime**, I wait for the **punishment**. 'One cabin point to Meagan for making her bed. Minus THREE for the rest of you,' she says.

'Minus **THREE?**' says Maisy.

'But Ginger has put on her shee–'

'Minus **THREE**. One for the unmade beds.
Half-made is not made. One for monkeying around.
And one for the bags. So you're on
minus four altogether.

Now, make
your beds
and
get to
lunch.'

I unroll my sleeping bag and put my pillow up onto the bed. I am disappointed I lost us a point for not finishing the job. **'Sorry, Meagan,'** I say.

Meagan pushes her glasses up her nose. 'That's okay,' she says. **'Let's just get ready for lunch.'**

Maisy and Meagan are quietly making their beds too. I am disappointed and tired. Too disappointed to remember Maisy and Martha's secret.

CHAPTER 3

Cabin four on
MINUS FOUR
troop down to lunch.

We eat lunch in a **BIG HALL**
with **plastic chairs** and
plastic tables
at the bottom of the hill.
The room smells like pine cleaner.
There is a long bench with a glass window and
built-in metal pots that are full of food.

'Food allergies?' asks a woman in
a white coat with a clipboard.

We all shake
our heads.
Nooooooooo.

'Well, you are fine to
go to the buffet,' she says.

We walk over to the buffet. **We are late.**

Every other kid is eating tinned spaghetti on toast.

You can always tell when spaghetti comes out of a

tin. It has a very different look from the spaghetti

that Italians eat, like the edges of the spaghetti

have been **SMUDGED**. I don't think any

Italian spaghetti looks like that.

'Tinned spaghetti. I **LOVE** tinned spaghetti,' shouts Maisy. Maisy helps herself to a big spoonful. Then another big spoonful and then another. There are three massive spoonfuls of spaghetti on Maisy's plate.

Martha copies Maisy.

'Maisy, you are hilarious,' says Martha.

Meagan looks at me. We both just take toast. 'I do not like spaghetti out of a can,' whispers Meagan.

'Me neither,' I say. 'I don't think Chaucer did either,' I add. Meagan laughs.

We carry our toast to a table. There is a pot of parmesan cheese powder on each table. Maisy offers it to Martha. Martha refuses.

Maisy pours the WHOLE pot on top of her spaghetti.

There is now more cheese than spaghetti.

Martha wrinkles her nose.

'That cheese powder has a funny smell,' she says.

**'It's parmesan and
I love it,'** shouts Maisy.

AS SHE SHOUTS, SHE PUFFS

CHEESE
POWDER

EVERYWHERE,
like a cheese-spraying **DRAGON.**

It lands all over the table like **dandruff.**

It lands on my toast. I put the toast down.
Parmesan powder smells a bit like vomit.

I do not want parmesan powder on my toast.

I especially do not want parmesan powder

sprayed out of Maisy's nose on my toast.

I look at Meagan.
Meagan pushes
her plate
away too.

For dessert there is ⋛**RED JELLY**.⋚
We never have red jelly at home. We never have jelly
at all because we don't get much dessert. Dessert
stopped when Mum entered her healthy-eating phase.
That phase has been going on for a **VERY** long time.

In fact, I can't remember actually ever having
dessert at lunchtime except on Christmas Day.
Dessert at lunchtime on a school day is incredible.

I help myself to the jelly and take my bowl back to
the table. Maisy, Martha and Meagan are already
there. I am just about to cut into my jelly when
Maisy reaches across the table and snatches it.

'**I love jelly,**' says Maisy.
She scoops up a massive spoonful of

MY JELLY.

'So do I,' I say reaching out my hand to snatch it back.

'Not as much as I do,' says Maisy, and scoops up the other half.

'Maisy, that was mine,' I say.

'I thought you didn't want it,' says Maisy.

'I didn't get the chance to not want it,' I say. 'You'd already eaten it.'

'Here, have mine,' says Meagan.

'I'll have it,' says Maisy, and reaches across the table.

'**No you won't,**' I say, and snatch it back.
'Thank you,' I say to Meagan.

'No problem,' says Meagan. 'I am not mad on red.'

'I **looooove** red,' says Maisy, jumping
up and down on her seat. 'Martha, we
should have red jelly at our secr–'

Martha looks up at Maisy and
gives her a look. Maisy goes quiet.
'Maisy, I know you LOVE red, but maybe you shouldn't
eat it,' Meagan says. 'Maybe it makes you a bit wild.'

'**A BIT WILD-ER,**' I add.

Maisy laughs and **THUMPS** the table.

'Once you have finished your lunch,

stack your dishes and head over to the

obstacle course,' says Mrs Cornell.

'OBSTACLE COURSE!'

shouts Maisy, and bolts towards the door quicker

than she ate my jelly.

'OBSTACLE COURSE!'

shouts Martha

and does ten

walkovers

to reach her.

Maisy is definitely not a good influence on Martha.

Maisy on red jelly is a SHOCKER.

I look at the two bowls they left on the table.
Cabin four is **already** on minus four points.

'Leave them,' says Meagan.

'But if we leave them, we'll lose cabin points,' I say.
'Can you even get lower than minus four?'

'Cabin four is going nowhere,' says Meagan. 'If we
pick up for Maisy and Martha they'll never learn.
If we pick up for Maisy and Martha they'll just get
their next cabin into trouble on **grade four** camp.'

Meagan has a point. I pick up the bowls anyway.
There is a big difference in my mind between
minus four and minus six. Two points.
But my love for Martha and
Maisy just dropped two points too.

We walk over to the obstacle course. It is the one we saw from the bus. There are lots of ropes at lots of different heights and it goes way up to four storeys high. There are rope bridges and platforms and tic-tac-toe planks. And lots of other obstacles too.

We have to work our way across and up a ladder to the next storey. We wear helmets and a harness. Our harnesses are connected by a clip to a wire above our heads. At the very end of the obstacle course you get to take a zip-line all the way to the bottom.

A ZIP-LINE IS A VERY LOOOOOOOOONG FLYING FOX.

Although **I love** flying foxes,
I am NOT feeling very positive about the
obstacle course. Neither is Meagan.
I am not feeling very positive because
who knows what Maisy and Martha
could do at four storeys high.
Maisy and Martha are

PRETTY CRAZY

on the ground. Maisy and
Martha are even crazier
on the ground with red jelly.
Who knows what will happen at four storeys?

**Who knows just how
many points cabin four
will lose?**

CHAPTER 4

We all head up onto the ropes in single file in our cabin groups. Ms Marinelli stands at the beginning of the rope course and helps us all on. Cabin four is pretty much **right in the middle** of the group. Four boys from cabin two are ahead of us.

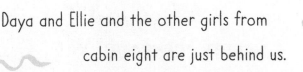

Daya and Ellie and the other girls from cabin eight are just behind us.

I feel a bit nervous even though the first part of the obstacle course is quite low. I stand on one rope and hold another rope above me to balance. Meagan follows me.

I follow right behind Maisy. Maisy follows Martha. Maisy and Martha are whispering about their secret again. I am getting a bit sick of this secret. No doubt it is going to involve gymnastics and no doubt we will lose **FORTY THOUSAND** cabin points because of it.

The boys ahead of Martha are being silly and start jumping on the rope.

'**Boys,**' calls Ms Marinelli. She is standing underneath us and looks as small as a midge from this high up.

Maisy ignores Ms Marinelli. 'That looks like fun,' says Maisy, and starts jumping too. Maisy shouts out the words to '**NINETY-NINE BOTTLES OF JUICE ON THE WALL**'

while she is jumping, only Maisy changes the words. '**NINETY-NINE BOTTLES OF JUICE ON A ROPE ...**'

I hold the rope above me tighter.

'Jumping up and down and singing silly songs,' says Ms Marinelli. I wait for it. 'No silly songs and games in the air. Minus two cabin points for cabin four.'

Maisy stops. Maisy loves singing and dancing but she also likes cabin points. Even though our new score of **MINUS SIX** for cabin four doesn't make that very obvious.

We all start to edge along the rope again. We cross a rope bridge and reach a platform with a ladder. We climb up to the next storey.

We are now pretty high up in the leaves of the trees. ⟿

'Just be careful. Put one foot after the other and **don't look down**,' says Ms Marinelli.

I am careful. We keep climbing. **I concentrate REALLY HARD** on putting one foot after the other. I concentrate really hard on not looking down. I concentrate really hard on trying to be sensible.

I climb over bits of wood. I climb across bridges. I climb through rope loops. But the **HIGHER** we get, the **SILLIER** Maisy and Martha get.

We climb up the last ladder onto the last storey.

Maisy and Martha are still in front of me.

We are now above the tree canopy.

I don't think I have **EVER** been this high.

I don't think I have looked down and seen

treetops that look like heads of broccoli

It is very **SCARY** and

very **VERY EXCITING**

all in the same breath.

Maisy starts jumping off the rope until she is just **hanging there**, held by her harness to the wire above our heads.

Maisy uses her strong muscles to flick back onto the rope.

OFF.

ON.

OFF.

ON.

Meanwhile, Martha starts using the rope like it is a **TIGHTROPE**.

She starts

JUMPING UP
and
BACKFLIPPING

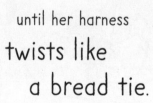

until her harness **twists like a bread tie.** Then she untwists it by flipping forwards.

Ms Marinelli sees Martha and Maisy.

'CABIN FOUR! NO JUMPING AND NO FLIPPING. STAY ON THE ROPE OR I WILL HAVE TO PULL YOU OFF. IT IS FOUR STOREYS HIGH AND IT IS DANGEROUS.'

Ms Marinelli is shouting, so her voice is faint. But even from up here I can hear her voice is quivering. I can tell Ms Marinelli is a bit concerned because she forgets to mention punishment. **She forgets to mention cabin points**. I can see why she is nervous. Maisy and Martha are pretty high up. We are all pretty high up. Nobody wants a kid to fall four storeys, even if they are a bit annoying.

I take a deep breath and concentrate. I watch my hands slide

along the rope. I concentrate on just

getting to
the end of the
obstacle course.

And then I stop.

I don't stop because I am scared. **I am.** I don't stop because I want to. I don't. I want to get through it and get off. I stop because I have to. I stop because Maisy and Martha have stopped. I stop because the boys ahead of Maisy and Martha have stopped too. I stop because there is a TRAFFIC JAM right up on the fourth storey of the obstacle course. Someone is all tangled.

'FOURTH STOREY,'

says Meagan just behind me.
'Why am I not surprised?

'I told you,' calls Ellie behind her.
'My grandmother is never wrong.'

THE ROPE UNDER OUR FEET STARTS TO WOBBLE.

'**Ahhh!**' screams Meagan,
and drops off the rope.

'AHHH!' scream the boys from cabin two, and drop off.

'AHHH!' I scream, and drop off.

'AHHH!' scream Daya and Ellie and the other girls from cabin eight, and they drop off too.

'AHHH!' screams Ms Marinelli from below when she looks up and sees what has happened.

She drops to the ground.

And there we are, all hanging from the wire like sneakers on a power line. Hanging from our harnesses and swinging, four storeys up in the air, with no way to move.

And far below,
Ms Marinelli is in a
DEAD FAINT.

oh no!

CHAPTER 5

I look down at Ms Marinelli. She is dead to the world **but hopefully not ACTUALLY** dead. All the other kids are looking too and they are quiet. So **quiet** that for the first time since we started climbing I can hear the birds.

I look up at Martha and Maisy. They are still on the rope above me and they are **not quiet**.

Martha is bouncing up and down on her bottom. Maisy is now kicking out to karate-chop leaves. **KA POW!**

Meagan looks at me. 'Martha should be able to get us out of this one.'

'And Martha will get us out of this one

if Maisy leads the way,' I say.

'Terrific,' says Meagan. 'Just terrific. You know things
are bad when Crazy Maisy is your best option.'
Meagan stops. 'But that's clever thinking, Ginger.'

I smile.

'MAISY!'

I shout.
'Maisy and
Martha,
you are going
to have to **help** us.

Nobody is as good at gym as either of you.'

Martha stops bouncing up and down on her bottom.

Martha has not noticed that the line has stopped.

She has not noticed that most of the kids are hanging

from the wire like POPPED BALLOONS. She

has not noticed that Ms Marinelli is **OUT COLD**.

Maisy stops
karate-chopping leaves
and looks around.

'Of course,'

says Maisy.

'Of course,'

says Martha.

But how will they get to the traffic

jam at the front of the line?

Everyone's harnesses are in the way!

This doesn't bother Maisy and Martha. They just unclip their own harnesses from the top wire, step around each kid, and then reclip them again.

It is very dangerous.

But they walk right to the front of the pile-up.

clever!

I am glad Ms Marinelli is in a dead faint. Ms Marinelli would certainly be in a dead faint if she saw Martha and Maisy unclip their harnesses.

poor Kai!

At the front of the pile-up is a boy called **Kai**. Kai has got himself in a knot.

A
BIG
KNOT.

He is tangled right up in a rope bridge and his shoelaces are tangled up with him.

All the other kids are banked up behind him.

'Step back
like this,'
says Maisy to Kai.

'And over →
this rope,'
says Martha.

'And over
← this one,'
says Maisy.

'And then back
over this one,' →
says Martha.

'Let me undo your shoe,' says Martha. 'And then you should be free.'

Martha takes off Kai's shoe. →

She holds it in her mouth and puts it back on once Kai's foot is free. Maisy ties up the shoelace.

'You'd have to be

CRAZY

to put Kai's shoe in your mouth,' says Meagan.

'Crazy is pretty incredible today,' I say.

I am **four storeys high** and **hanging by a wire** but I know Maisy and Martha have got this. **I should be scared.** I should be **DEAD** scared. I should even be like Ms Marinelli and possibly be dead on the forest floor. But in a crazy wild way, I trust Maisy. In a crazy wild way I trust Martha too.

Maisy looks back at Martha. 'You stay here to lead the way,' says Maisy. 'I'll go back to the others.'

Maisy and Martha work as a **perfect team**. Maisy jumps back over Kai and Martha and turns round to the boys from cabin two. Martha stands on the rope and Maisy sits on the rope next to her.

'**Grab my foot**,' Maisy calls to each boy.

Once the boys have pulled themselves up using Maisy's foot, Martha helps them stand.

Except **Max R,** who is a **bit sniffy** and does it himself.

Then Maisy comes over to me. 'Heave yourself up,' Maisy says to me and then Meagan.

Maisy's foot is strong.

I get back up on top of the rope and then Maisy gives me a hand to stand up. I grab hold of the rope above me so I can get my balance.

Maisy then jumps around us and pulls up Ellie, Daya and the rest of cabin eight.

Maisy is **fearless** on the rope. She is *fast* and **fearless** and very, **very calm**. She is calm despite the fact we are four storeys high. She is calm despite the fact her harness is unclipped. She is calm despite the fact she has eaten two **RED JELLIES**. She is calm even though Ms Marinelli is in a dead faint and **COULD IN FACT ACTUALLY BE DEAD**. She is calm and kind.

'I'll stay at the back,' Maisy yells to Martha. 'You stay at the front and lead the group.'

We make our way across the last bridge, the one Kai got tangled in, following Martha. We jump across to the final platform and then we take the zip-line all the way to the bottom.

IZZZZ

ALL
THE WAY
DOWN.

My legs and arms are shaking. I am so excited to be back on ground that does not **WOBBLE**.

Maisy stays up on the platform to make sure everybody is safe. Mrs Cornell has now appeared with three more cabins.

She has her arm around Ms Marinelli. Ms Marinelli is standing up and rubbing her head. **She looks a bit green.**

'That was really admirable,' says Ms Marinelli to Martha. 'You and Maisy were fabulous. We would have been very stuck with the lot of you up there.'

'Not as stuck as us,' I say.

Ms Marinelli laughs. 'I might have been in a dead faint, but I still know that's worth **TEN** cabin points,' she says to Martha.

'Really?' says Martha. 'That takes us to four points!'

Martha is very good at maths when it comes to cabin points.

'If you felt a bit queasy earlier,' says Meagan, 'you'd better not look up there.'

I look up. I look up and see
Maisy. I look up and see
Maisy dancing on the
small platform where the
zip-line starts.
She is dancing
in her **undies**
on the platform.

'Dancing on the platform in
spotty undies,' calls Mrs Cornell.
I wait for the punishment.
'Maisy Brown, down now.'

Maisy!

Maisy goes
to pull her ➔
undies down.

'NOT YOUR UNDIES. YOU,'

calls Ms Marinelli. 'Your good behaviour

has just earned cabin four **ten points.**

I would be very sad to take them away again.'

'WHEEEEEEEE,'

says Maisy as she

zips down the line.

'Ten points!

That is cool.'

'Not as cool as you must be,' says Mrs Cornell.

'It's about four degrees. Get your clothes on!'

Later that night, Ms Marinelli pours warm soup into a cup. When you are cold and tired, nothing tastes better than **tomato soup**. Even if you do not really like vegetables. I must remember to recommend it to Lottie for after her tonsils are out. Tomato soup would be very easy to eat with a sore throat.

'Can I have another cup please?' asks Martha.

Maisy kicks Martha under the table. Maisy kicks Martha so hard the table **WOBBLES**.

'Actually, I forgot I'm not hungry,' says Martha.

Martha looks at Maisy

and **winks**.

'I don't know what secret language Martha and Maisy speak, but they were superb today,' says Ms Marinelli. 'You all were. **Three cheers for cabin four.'**

'Four cheers,' I say. 'Four of us.

'**FOUR** cheers for cabin four!'

'Four might be an unlucky number,' says Ellie, 'but we were very lucky to have cabin four with us today.'

Ms Marinelli smiles.

In the end we didn't win the cabin points.

In fact, we came fourth.

It is hard to make up cabin points when you start a **MILLION** points behind. But while winning the cabin points would have been nice, I would never have traded Maisy or Martha or even Meagan for anything.

Maisy and Martha are

RULE-BREAKERS.

Meagan is a **goody-goody**. The thing

about rule-breakers is that they are brilliant at

remembering to bring snacks for a midnight feasts

and even pretty good

at keeping the midnight

feast a secret.

And the thing about clever **goody-goodies** like Meagan is that even though they are goody-goodies they are **clever enough** to work out secrets.

They are also very good at coming up with places to hide secret midnight feasts – places that are **so secret**, you never ever get caught.

There was no best friend at Star Glen Ranch. There was no **horse-riding, wild buffalos** and no **lassos** either. But there were **FARTY BEDS** and there was **RED JELLY** and an **obstacle course**. And in the end there were four friends, three of whom started with M.

There were three friends who went to bed with chocolate on their breath and one who went to bed smelling like

chocolate
and
toothpaste.

guess who?

Cabin four **DID NOT WIN** the cabin points, but cabin four **HAD A BALL**. Number four is not such an unlucky number after all.

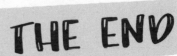

THE END

HOW TO HAVE THE
LUCKIEST
CAMP
EVER!

HOW TO SNEAK A
Midnight Feast
INTO CAMP

Midnight feasts are always forbidden on camp.
They are just one of those things grown-ups won't
let kids do. But if you can have a **midnight feast**
with a friend who doesn't have
any food allergies, **there is
nothing better**.

But the big question is:
where to hide the food?

The torch!

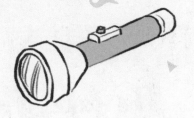

Torches are always allowed on camp but **NOBODY** ever uses them, because the camp's lights are always on.

So unscrew the torch, tip out the batteries and **VOILA**, you have the **perfect spot** to hide a midnight feast. Make sure you wrap the lollies before you hide them inside the torch.

Remember, the bigger the torch, the bigger the batteries — which means **the bigger the bag of lollies!**

The fake slipper toe!

You will need two mini chocolate bars and a big pair of slippers for this one — maybe your mum or dad's slippers.

The bigger the slipper, the bigger the midnight feast!

Push a mini chocolate bar into the toe of each slipper. Cover with cotton wool.

WARNING

Do not wear the slippers near the camp fire

until AFTER you have had your midnight feast.

Otherwise, the chocolates could melt

and your toes will be **CACTUS**.

WARNING

Do not use smelly old slippers.

Those chocolate bars might be wrapped but if the

slippers smell like cheesy feet, so will your chocolate!

The hollow book!

Hollow books have actually been around for EVER. They used to store **poison** or **jewels** or **keys** to secret compartments. From the outside, a hollow book looks just like a normal book.

You need a really thick book for this.

First, glue the back pages to the back cover.

Glue the back few pages together.

Starting on page nine, and with help from a grown-up, carve out a hole in the pages using a craft knife.

You will only be able
to carve through a
few pages at a time.

Just be patient
and keep carving until the hole is as big and as
deep as you want it to be.

When you're finished, keep the whole thing together
with a rubber band, and add a bookmark for extra
authenticity.

WARNING

**Do not choose a book
that belongs to your sister**
that she has not finished reading yet.
I did that and Violet nearly **KILLED** me.

Rules for midnight feasts

Plan ahead if possible, so that everyone who will be at the midnight feast can bring some food along.

But make sure everyone keeps it a <u>secret</u>. Maisy and Martha were not that great at keeping our midnight feast a secret!

If you are going to share your food, make sure you don't share it with friends who have **allergies**.

If you absolutely must share your food with a friend who has allergies, make sure you clear it with his/her mum, dad or carer first.

And remember, NEVER EVER bring anything with NUTS in it.

They get stuck in your teeth anyway, which is a dead giveaway for the morning. And they are way too healthy for a midnight feast.

Midnight feasts should be JUNKY.

HOW TO
have fun
ON THE BUS

In my experience of one camp and Violet's experience of three camps, school camps **always** involve a bus.

Buses are **INCREDIBLY** boring.

Sometimes they put on a video but usually you can't hear it unless you are sitting in the front two rows.

It is really fun to make up the words to whatever is happening on the screen. So, you and a friend can each choose a character on the telly. If there is a police officer arresting a baddie, for example, you could say something like this:

 **OFFICER**: Mr Crisper, we have finally caught you, you dangerous, ruthless, villainous crim.

MR CRISPER: Officer Bandy Legs, I am an innocent rabbit. I did not steal the carrots.

 **OFFICER**: Then why is there carrot between your two front teeth?

MR CRISPER: I AM A RABBIT. That was breakfast.

 **OFFICER**: I knew it! And you have carrots in your fridge.

MR CRISPER: Of course I have carrots in my fridge. I am a rabbit!

 OFFICER: So who stole the carrots?

MR CRISPER: Somebody on a health kick. Start with Ginger Green's mum.

HOW TO PLAY
Numberplate
BINGO!

Now the idea of this one is easy, but be warned,
I have never actually seen anybody win.

You have to spot the numberplate from **every
state and territory.** So, if you're in Australia
you need to find an example of at least one
numberplate each from:

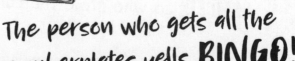
The person who gets all the
numberplates yells **BINGO!**

How to sing along!

I know I made fun of Meagan and her perfect harmonies but Megan is clever and therefore she knows that when you sing, a trip goes faster. You don't have to be able to do perfect harmonies when you sing, either!

'99 Bottles of Juice' is a good one because it gives you a focus and you can even mix it up a bit.

You can also count those bottles of juice backwards in twos **(99, 97, 95...)** or threes **(99, 96, 93...)** – but you have to be good at mental maths!

SICK OF JUICE? How about '99 Bottles of Sunscreen', '99 Cartons of Choc Milk' or even '99 Cans of Baked Beans'?

HOW TO MAKE
bus bags

This is my very favourite activity so I have saved it until last. If you have to drive quite a long way, work out where you are going. Work out which towns or turn-offs you will go past to get there. **Maps are really helpful for this.**

For every major turn-off or town you will pass through on the way to camp, get a bag or an envelope. Put in a little note for your bus partner, along with something else, like a **puzzle** or a **poem** or a **scratch'n'sniff sticker** or even a piece of **bubblegum.**

On the front of the bag write
when or where to open it. →

When your friend gets to the turn-off
that's written on the envelope or bag,

they open it and enjoy the surprise.

You could even organise
to do it with a friend before
you go so that you get your
own bus bags!